Little Sister
and the
Month Brothers

Little Sister
and the
Month Brothers

RETOLD BY BEATRICE SCHENK DE REGNIERS

PICTURES BY MARGOT TOMES

A MULBERRY PAPERBACK BOOK · NEW YORK

Text copyright © 1976 by Beatrice Schenk de Regniers.
Pictures copyright © 1976 by Margot Tomes.

Printed in the United States of America.

10 9 8 7 6 5 4 3 2 1

First published in 1976 by Clarion Books.

Library of Congress Cataloging-in-Publication Data
De Regniers, Beatrice Schenk.
Little Sister and the Month Brothers / retold by Beatrice Schenk de Regniers;
pictures by Margot Tomes. p. cm.
Summary: A retelling of the Slavic fairy tale in which the Month Brothers' magic helps Little Sister
fulfill seemingly impossible tasks which prove the undoing of her greedy stepmother and stepsister.
[1 Fairy tales. 2. Folklore—Slavic countries.] I. Tomes, Margot, ill. II. Title. PZ8.D45L1 1994
[398.2]—dc20 [E] 93-44053 CIP AC

First Mulberry Edition, 1994. Published by arrangement with the author
and with the illustrator's estate.

ISBN 0-688-13633-8

for LFC with love

Well, there was this girl. We don't know her name, but everyone called her Little Sister. Her mother was dead, and so was her father. She lived with her stepmother and stepsister in a little cottage near a dark forest.

This was once upon a time, in the days when stepmothers were wicked and stepsisters were mean and lazy.

wash wash wash

sweep sweep sweep

scrub scrub scrub

cook cook cook

spin spin spin

stitch stitch stitch

Little Sister had to do all the work in the house.

She had to do all the work outside the house too—in the meadow and in the garden. And every morning and every evening, she milked the cow.

The stepmother and the stepsister never said thank you to Little Sister. All day long they hollered and they grumbled and they complained.

Tra la la
Tra la la

But Little Sister did not seem to mind. Most of the time she sang or hummed while she worked. And every day Little Sister grew prettier and prettier.

tra

la

la

When Little Sister looks so happy and so pretty, it somehow makes *you* look rather mean and ugly.

The stepmother and stepsister couldn't stand seeing Little Sister looking happier and prettier day after day.

What if a young man were to come by? He might choose Little Sister for a wife instead of the step-sister!

The stepmother and stepsister made up their minds to get rid of Little Sister.

The stepsister looked out of the window. It was bitter cold outside. Snow covered the ground. Now the stepsister knew how to get rid of Little Sister! She would send her out in the cold to look for fresh violets.

The stepmother thought this was a very good idea. She pushed Little Sister outside and told her not to come back without fresh violets. Then she slammed the door shut and locked it. Poor Little Sister did not even have a coat on.

Brrr

I'm frozen.
I can't go
one more
step.

A light!

Courage!
I must go on.

How cold it was. Just when Little Sister thought she could not take one more step, she saw a light shining high above the trees. She walked toward the light.

Courage!
I must climb
this rock.

Soon she reached a huge rock. She could see that the light came from a fire burning way on top. She managed to climb the rock.

Twelve men were standing in a circle around a big fire. Three of the men had long white hair and long white beards. They wore fur capes, white as snow.

Three were very young men—almost boys. One of them wore a brown velvet cape lined with green silk. The other two were dressed all in green. Three were full-grown men. They looked tall and strong, and their capes were of green and gold. The last three men had brown beards and wore woolen capes of gold and brown.

Little Sister knew at once that these were the twelve Month Brothers.

Oh! These must be the Month Brothers.

Brother January asked Little Sister what she wanted. Very politely, Little Sister asked if she could come near the fire and warm herself. Then she explained that she had come to gather violets, and that she dare not go home without them.

Hmm. Brothers,
we must help
Little Sister.

Brother January told the Month Brothers they
must all help Little Sister.

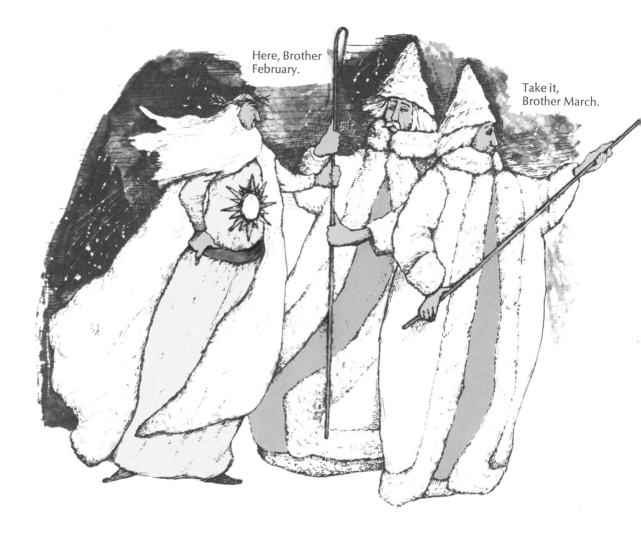

January passed his staff to Brother February. An icy wind began to blow. Quickly February gave the staff to a young man standing next to him.

Brother April,
only you can
give us violets.

As March held the staff, the snow melted on the ground, and a patch of muddy earth could be seen. Soon there was a hint of green grass.

March smiled and said to the young man next to him, dressed all in green from head to toe: "Take the staff, Brother April. Only you can give us violets."

Brother April took the staff and whirled it above his head. There was a shower of warm rain. Then all the tree branches nearby put out green leaves.

Grass appeared, and the muddy brown earth turned green.

Hurry, Little Sister. Gather your violets.

Thank you! Thank you very much.

Now, in a circle around Brother April, there was a carpet of blue violets.

Little Sister quickly filled her apron with the sweet-smelling violets. She thanked the Month Brothers and ran home.

Open the door!
Open the door!

Violets!

Hurry and milk
the cow. You're
late.

Yes,
Stepmother.

Hmm.

When Little Sister brought home the violets, the stepmother and stepsister were astonished. The sweet smell of violets filled the house. But no one thanked Little Sister. The stepmother told her to get back to work. The stepsister was thinking of a way to get rid of Little Sister.

The next day, the stepsister waited until supper was over and it was dark outside. Then she told Little Sister to go out and gather fresh strawberries. The stepmother gave Little Sister a basket and pushed her out the door. She told her not to come back until the basket was filled with strawberries.

Brrr

Courage!

Little Sister ran to keep from freezing. At last she
reached the rock and climbed it.

The Month Brothers were there, standing in a circle around the fire. Little Sister greeted them politely and told them why she had come.

Once more the staff was passed—from January to February, from February to March to April to May, and at last to Brother June.

As the staff went from Month Brother to Month Brother, once again the seasons changed and the earth became green and blossoming.

Hurry, Little Sister.
You may gather five
berries. Then it will
be winter again.

Thank you.
Thank you very much.

Little Sister saw the white, star-shaped blossoms
appear in the green grass—and fade. Then she saw
the green berries grow and ripen to red.

June warned Little Sister to hurry. He told her
she could gather five berries.

Quickly Little Sister gathered the berries, thanked
the Month Brothers, and ran home.

The stepmother and stepsister looked at the basket greedily. When they saw only five strawberries, they were angry.

They would not believe Little Sister when she told them the Month Brothers would not let her pick more than five berries.

The stepsister and stepmother ate the five strawberries, one after the other. They had never tasted anything so delicious!

The stepsister made up her mind to get a basket full of those delicious strawberries. She put on her fur-lined cape and hood. She put on her fur-lined boots and her fur-lined mittens, and she ran out to find the Month Brothers.

Brrr.

That must be the fire
of the Month Brothers.

Even with all her warm clothes the stepsister
began to feel cold. When she saw the light, she ran
toward it and climbed the rock.

She pushed her way past the Month Brothers to warm herself at the fire. When January asked why she had come, the stepsister told him it was none of his business. She said she would speak only to Brother June.

January was angry. He swung his staff in the air. The wind blew. The snow fell thick and fast.

The stepsister could no longer see the fire or the Month Brothers. She stumbled along in the snow, trying to find her way home.

I'm worried. Where could my darling be?

I must find her.

The stepmother, waiting at home, was worried.
At last she decided to go out to look for the stepsister.

They must be lost forever.

Little Sister waited and waited for the step-mother and the stepsister to come home. But they never came back. No one ever saw them again.

Now Little Sister had the cottage to herself, and the garden and the meadow and the cow.

wash wash wash

sweep sweep sweep

scrub scrub scrub

cut cut cut

dig dig dig

chop chop chop

Good Daisy!

Hold still, Daisy.

Little Sister worked as hard as ever. But now there was no one to holler or grumble or complain.

The only sound in the house was the sound of Little Sister singing to herself. She was lonely sometimes.

One day an honest farmer came to the door and asked Little Sister to marry him, and she did.

cut cut cut

cut cut cut

chop chop chop

chop chop chop

dig dig dig

dig dig dig

Hold still, Daisy.

Now it's my turn.
Good Daisy.

Little Sister was no longer lonely. The farmer was very fond of her, and he helped her with the work.

Sometimes the farmer hollered or grumbled or complained, but not very often.

Sometimes, on snowy winter evenings, Little Sister would look out of the window and remember the twelve Month Brothers.

And the Month Brothers never forgot Little Sister. The spring flowers came early to the meadow. And the fruits and vegetables in the garden were always the first and the finest. In the wintertime, the snow drifted into a wall around the house and garden to protect them from the cold wind.

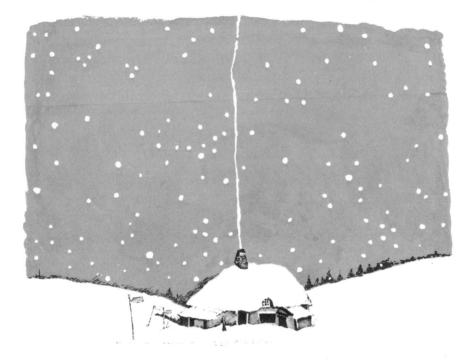

All went well for Little Sister and her husband, and
they lived together in peace and happiness.

Author's Note

I remember this story of the Month Brothers from my childhood. And later, when my sister and I came home for midterm vacations, it was my mother's pleasure to offer us fresh strawberries. Fresh strawberries in February? In Crawfordsville, Indiana? Where could she have found them? I knew. "Oh," I would say, "I see you have been to the Month Brothers!"

This is a Slavic tale, and the heroine's name is usually Marushka or some variation of that. But it pleases me to call her Little Sister and so relate her more closely to the chthonic brothers.

Over the years the story has taken on more and more meaning for me, and my perception of it changes as my perception of life changes—from sentimental to romantic to poetic to ironic to faintly comic, layer upon layer. (I am unwilling to give up any of them.) And now I offer this story to new readers.